INGER and LASSE SANDBERG

Translated by Judy Abbott Maurer

Dusty
Wants to Help

R&S
BOOKS

Stockholm   New York   Toronto   London

Rabén & Sjögren Stockholm

Text copyright © 1983 by Inger Sandberg
Illustrations copyright © 1983 by Lasse Sandberg
Translation copyright © 1987 by Judy Abbott Maurer
All rights reserved
Library of Congress catalog card number: 87-45160
Originally published in Swedish under the title *Hjälpa till, sa Pulvret*
by Rabén & Sjögren, 1983
Printed in Italy
First American edition, 1987
ISBN 91 29 583365

R&S Books are distributed in the United States by Farrar, Straus & Giroux, New York,
in the UK by Ragged Bears, Andover,
and in Canada by Methuen Publications, Toronto, Ontario.

"Would you look after Dusty for a little while?"
Dusty's mother asks her father.
He is Dusty's grandpa.

"All right," says Grandpa.
"I'm just about to make some pancakes."
"I want to help," cries Dusty,
running into the kitchen.
He pushes a chair over to Grandpa
and climbs up.
He finds three eggs.
"Hold it," says Grandpa.
"The eggs are supposed to go into the bowl."

"I want to help," says Dusty,
as he drops two eggs into the bowl.
The third one cracks in his hand.
"Oh boy, what a mess," says Grandpa.
"There will be eggshells in the pancakes.
I'll have to take them out."

"I want to help," says Dusty,
swishing his hands in the egg mixture.
"No, no, no!" says Grandpa.
His voice is getting louder.
He wipes Dusty's hands
and lifts him down to the floor.

"I want to help," says Dusty.
"Not with the eggs," says Grandpa.
"Not with the eggs," says Dusty.
Grandpa hurries to add the flour,
milk, and new eggs — without the shells.

11

"Please don't touch anything,"
says Grandpa.
"Don't touch," says Dusty,
as he presses a switch on the mixer.
The beater and the bowl begin
whirling around.
Flour flies all over.
Grandpa shouts, "No, no, no!"

13

"Enough help. You'll have to stay on the floor now," says Grandpa. "I have to fry the pancakes." "I want to help," says Dusty. "No," says Grandpa. "Can I have some milk?" asks Dusty, pushing the chair closer to the bowl. "Are you thirsty? Here is a cup of milk," says Grandpa.

15

Then Grandpa pours some batter
into the frying pan,
and Dusty pours all of his milk
into the batter.
"No, no, no, no!
I am going crazy!" shouts Grandpa.
He puts Dusty on the floor again.

"I want to help," says Dusty.
"Why don't you play with your train?"
suggests Grandpa.
"I have to watch the pancakes."
"Or else?" asks Dusty.
"Or else there will be no food to eat,"
says Grandpa.
"Go play with your train and little men."

19

So Dusty finds his train
and eight little men,
and he sets the table with them.
He puts one little man in each glass
— one, two, three.
One little man in the butter,
one little man in the jam,
and one little man in the sugar bowl!
On each plate he puts a train car.

When Dusty's mother returns,
Dusty is so excited
that he throws two little men high up
into the air.
Where did they go?

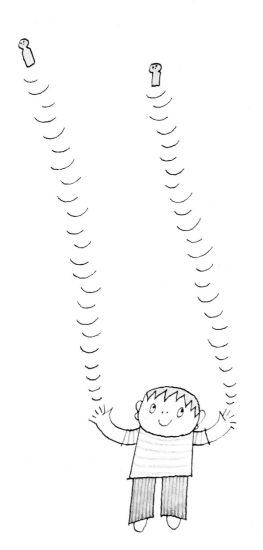

23

"Something smells delicious,"
says Dusty's mother.
"Have you been a good boy
and helped your grandpa?"
"I want to help," says Dusty,
pushing the chair AGAIN.
"Don't come back in here!"
shouts Grandpa.
"No more help, please!
Let's sit down and eat."

When they sit down at the table,
they find one little man in each glass
— one, two, three . . .
one little man in the butter — four . . .

one little man in the sugar — five . . .

one little man in the jam — six . . .

one little man in a pancake — seven . . .

Dusty had eight little men with his train.
Where is the eighth?

Dusty knows.
But he's not telling!